Ecosystems
Grasslands

by Nadia Higgins

Bullfrog Books

Ideas for Parents and Teachers

Bullfrog Books let children practice reading informational text at the earliest reading levels. Repetition, familiar words, and photo labels support early readers.

Before Reading

• Discuss the cover photo. What does it tell them?

• Look at the picture glossary together. Read and discuss the words.

Read the Book

• "Walk" through the book and look at the photos. Let the child ask questions. Point out the photo labels.

• Read the book to the child, or have him or her read independently.

After Reading

• Prompt the child to think more. Ask: Have you ever visited a grassland? Have you seen videos or pictures? How would you describe it?

Bullfrog Books are published by Jump!
5357 Penn Avenue South
Minneapolis, MN 55419
www.jumplibrary.com

Library of Congress Cataloging-in-Publication Data

Names: Higgins, Nadia, author.
Title: Grasslands / by Nadia Higgins.
Description: Minneapolis, MN: Jump!, Inc., [2017]
Series: Ecosystems
Audience: Ages 5–8. | Audience: K to grade 3.
Includes bibliographical references and index.
Identifiers: LCCN 2016056976 (print)
LCCN 2016057729 (ebook)
ISBN 9781620316795 (hardcover: alk. paper)
ISBN 9781620317327 (pbk.)
ISBN 9781624965562 (ebook)
Subjects: LCSH: Grassland ecology—Juvenile literature. | Grasslands—Juvenile literature.
Classification: LCC QH541.5.P7 H525 2017 (print)
LCC QH541.5.P7 (ebook) | DDC 577.4—dc23
LC record available at https://lccn.loc.gov/2016056976

Editor: Jenny Fretland VanVoorst
Book Designer: Molly Ballanger
Photo Researcher: Molly Ballanger

Photo Credits: Dreamstime: Mikael Males, 20–21. iStock: lightpix, 5, 23tm. Shutterstock: Jo Ann Snover, cover; Amy Nichole Harris, 1; Nancy Bauer, 3; Pindyurin Vasily, 4; Eduard Kyslynskyy, 6–7; Yurich, 8; Brian Lasenby, 9; Gil.K, 10–11, 23tr; zahorec, 12–13; GUDKOV ANDREY, 17; robert_s, 23tl; jordache, 23bl; Viktor1, 23bm; Moisieiev Igor, 23br; Giedriius, 24. SuperStock: Bernd Rohrschneider/FLPA, 14–15; imageBROKER, 16; Stephen Dalton/Minden Pictures, 18–19.

Printed in the United States of America at Corporate Graphics in North Mankato, Minnesota.

Table of Contents

Big Sky

The land is flat.

The sky looks huge.

Grass sways in the wind.
This is a grassland.

Few trees grow here.
But there is lots of grass.
It can grow very tall!

Some grasslands
have seasons.

These are prairies.

Winters are icy.

Summers sizzle.

Other grasslands
are always hot.

These are savannas.

One season is dry.

Another season brings rain.

Grasslands are home
to many animals.
The animals feed
on the grass.

They eat up one spot.

Then they move
to a new one.

nest

In winter, the grass dies off.

Some animals do not eat.

They make nests.

They rest.

In spring,
new grass grows.

Where Are the Grasslands?

The Great Plains of North America were once covered in wild grass. Today, the land is mostly farms. Wheat and corn grow for miles.

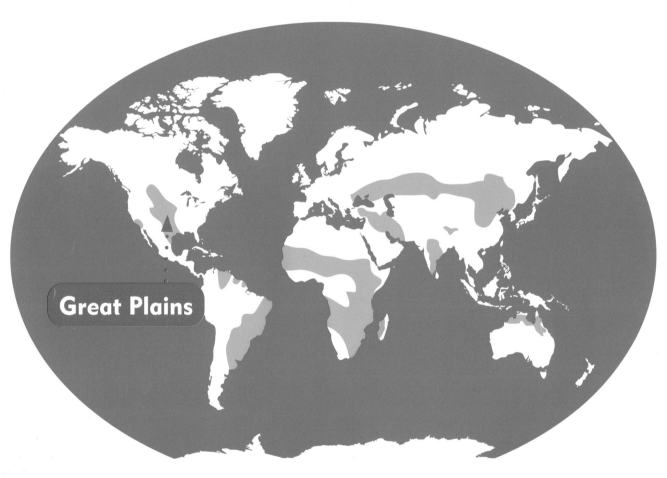

Great Plains

■ grassland

Picture Glossary

grass
A kind of plant with long, thin leaves.

prairies
Flat, nearly treeless grasslands that experience seasonal changes in climate.

savannas
Grassy plains with few or no trees found in a tropical area.

seasons
Periods of the year marked by certain kinds of weather.

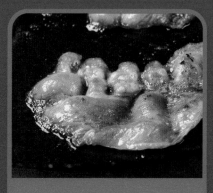

sizzle
Hiss with heat, as if burning or frying.

sways
Gently moves back and forth.

Index

To Learn More

Finding more information is as easy as 1, 2, 3.

❶ Go to www.factsurfer.com

❷ Enter "grasslands" into the search box.

❸ Choose your book to see a list of websites.